To my son Michael Scott Wilson III:
Mom says thanks for growing into such a fine young man.
All my love—K. W.

To Dylan and Jacob—J. C.

MARGARET K. McELDERRY BOOKS
An imprint of Simon & Schuster Children's Publishing Division
1230 Avenue of the Americas, New York, New York 10020
Text copyright © 2012 by Karma Wilson
Illustrations copyright © 2012 by Jane Chapman
All rights reserved, including the right of reproduction in whole or in part in any form.
MARGARET K. McELDERRY BOOKS is a trademark of Simon & Schuster, Inc.
For information about special discounts for bulk purchases,
please contact Simon & Schuster Special Sales
at 1-866-506-1949 or business@simonandschuster.com.
The Simon & Schuster Speakers Bureau can bring authors to your live event.
For more information or to book an event, contact the Simon & Schuster Speakers Bureau at 1-866-248-3049
or visit our website at www.simonspeakers.com.
Book design by Lauren Rille
The text for this book is set in Adobe Caslon.
The illustrations for this book are rendered in acrylic paint.
Manufactured in China
0418 SCP
8 10 9
Library of Congress Cataloging-in-Publication Data
Wilson, Karma.
Bear says thanks / Karma Wilson ; illustrations by Jane Chapman. — 1st ed.
p. cm.
Summary: Bear thanks his friends for bringing food dishes to his dinner party and finds
a way of sharing something of his own.
ISBN 978-1-4169-5856-7 (hardcover : alk. paper)
ISBN 978-1-4424-6126-0 (eBook)
[1. Gratitude—Fiction. 2. Sharing—Fiction. 3. Bears—Fiction. 4. Forest animals—Fiction.]
I. Chapman, Jane, 1970– ill. II. Title.
PZ7.W69656Be 2012
[E]—dc23
2011026112

Bear Says Thanks

Karma Wilson

illustrations by Jane Chapman

MARGARET K. MCELDERRY BOOKS

New York   London   Toronto   Sydney   New Delhi

All alone in his cave,
Bear listens to the wind.
He is bored,
bored,
bored . . .
and he misses his friends.

"I could make a big dinner!
A feast I could share."

But he looks through his cupboard,
and the cupboard is bare.

Then Mouse stops by with a huckleberry pie.

And the bear says, "Thanks!"

Bear says, "Goodness me,
a delectable pie!"

"But I have made nothing,"
he adds with a sigh.

Then they hear, "Hi ho!"
and they both see Hare
with a big batch of muffins
at the door of the lair!

Hare hurries in from the cold, rushing wind . . .

and the **bear**
says,
"Thanks!"

"Of course!" says Hare.
Then he points to the door.

"Here comes Badger.
He's got even more!"

"Brrrrr!" says Badger
as he tromps inside.
He sets down his pole
and he smiles real wide.

"I'm back from a stroll at the old fishin' hole!"

And the bear
says,
"Thanks!"

Then Gopher and Mole
tunnel up from the ground.
"We have warm honey nuts.
Let's pass them around!"

There's a flap and a flitter
and a flurry in the den
when in flutters Owl
with Raven and Wren.

"We have pears from the tree
and herbs to brew tea!"

And the bear
says,
"Wait . . ."

Bear mutters and he stutters
and he wears a big frown.
Bear sighs and he moans
and he plops himself down.

"You have brought yummy treats!
You are so nice to share.
But me, I have nothing.
My cupboards are bare!"

Mouse squeaks, "Don't fret.
There's enough, dear Bear.
You don't need any food,
you have stories to share!"

His friends hug him tight. "It will be all right!"

And the bear says, "Thanks!"

They lay out their feast
on a quilt on the ground.
And the bear takes a seat
while his friends gather round.

In a cave in the woods,
in a warm, bright lair,
the friends feel grateful
for their good friend Bear.

They pass around platters.
They tweet and they chatter . . .

and they all say, "Thanks!"